CHAPTER ONE – A HERO IS
AND WE MEET HIM WHE

Justice. The word alone is, no wa
Shit. Well so much for a grand, sweeping opening. You know what, fuck it, fuck it all, stupid fucking fuck!

Ok, and breathe. I'm fine. I never could let the little things go. I've always had to sweat the small stuff, a trait that never won me many friends (but sure lost me a lot of them). I guess that's how I ended up here; little things, niggling at me, like a stone, slowly gathering moss as it picks up speed growing bigger and bigger, until finally that little rock gets to the bottom of the hill and smashes you in the balls.

I suppose I should tell you a little about myself. I'm a superhero, or so I'm told. A reluctant superhero at best, I never really got on board with the whole "saving the world" bullshit, and never really got on board with the whole "looking out for the little guy" crap either. Basically I'm just a guy who had the misfortune to be in the wrong lab at the wrong time when the wrong experiment went wrong.

Most guys would be thrilled to have my abilities: I'm fast, I'm strong *and* I can climb walls. I guess my main beef with this superhero malarkey started right at the beginning. You see, I got bitten by a radioactive spider.

I know, right?

Talk about your painfully obvious cliché! I'll tell you about it some other time, but here was my main beef: got bitten by a spider, got the abilities of a spider… so what was I supposed to call myself? Unfortunately Spiderman pretty much took my gig and with it any chance of having a cool superhero name.

Plus these days what with every superhero needing to be registered, before I could legally use any of my newly acquired powers not only did I have to decide if I was going to register with either the SIA (Superhero Intelligence Agency) or the VBI (Villains and Badmen Industries), but I also had to pick out a name. And so I was stuck, I could go all shitty and call myself Manspider, but Jesus, who would respect that guy? All I know is his name and already I wanna punch the guy. I did think about naming myself after the spider that bit me, but Lesser-spotted-labiamite-man just didn't seem to roll of the tongue, plus in a world already full of 'something-mans' going down that route seemed a bit too cliché (no offence Something-Man).

It took a lot of soul searching and long walks in the park (well... a half bottle of scotch and a flick through a children's illustrated encyclopaedia) to settle on the name ARACHNO. Of course the other option was The Arachno, but then I'd have to refer to myself in the third person, and that's just something Arachno refuses to do. Heh. Plus when filling in forms is that a title or a first name? More trouble than it's worth. Also every time you meet someone they'll be like 'Hey! The Arachno! Can I call you *Arachno*?' Pfft! I hate people. That's another one of my flaws, but there's plenty of time for that.

So anyway, where was I? I'm very easily distracted. Oh yeah, and so I found myself, 3 days after my accident, standing outside the registry office. My name ready, my 100 bucks processing fee (rip off much Mr President?) and no clue which agency I was going to join. It was a tough choice. On one hand, the evil guys do generally lose, but they get to live like a boss: prostitutes and drugs and all that jazz until they get caught, pretty cool. Whereas the heroes are supposed to be role models, someone people can look up to, yuck. Still, I could be one of those vigilante-types: never seen, the fear in the back of the law breaker's mind and yada yada yada all that Batman bullshit.

I could do the whole villain spiel, I thought. Although villains spend a LOT of time thinking about, and working on, big evil schemes to take over the world or how to kill their protagonist and generally working hard to ruin superheroes' lives and making people really hate you, and frankly, that just ain't me. I like to clock out, get out and zone out with my cock out of an evening. Plus the new season of *Game of Thrones* was starting soon.

Decision made. I was joining the SIA, I was going to be a (rather lazy) superhero.

CHAPTER TWO – (THE HOME OF A HERO)

When I'm not 'busy', out making the world a safer place, people call me Joe. Joe Jacobs. As soon as my parents gave me an alliterated name I should've known I'd end up here sooner or later. I guess I just had other dreams. I never dreamt of being the guy people depended on, the guy people wanted around. I wanted to be the guy everyone left alone, the guy people didn't mind being around but were quite happy either way. I never wanted to leave my mark on the world, I didn't want to make any marks anywhere. I'm quite a tidy person, in fact.

I never buy more stuff than I need, never buy less (or more) than two ply, never buy a new costume if I can get my mum to sew the hole in the crotch. I don't know what it is about tights, but they always seem to split at the crotch for me. Oh, that's another thing I hate about being a superhero: tights. I mean they look bad enough on a fat drunk girl in a tiny skirt throwing up behind McDonalds on a Saturday night. But me? I'm a reasonably stout, usually drunk, self-conscious bloke with a few proportions I'd rather leave to the imagination. Stupid government-regulated costumes. In the old days it was fine: you wanted to wear a nappy and a gimp mask, that was fine.

But then we privatised. Terrible move. Now everything has to go through an official board. Seriously, if I wanted to add, for example, an 'I Love NY' badge to my costume it would take at least three weeks before it was ok'd. And while I'm at it, no-one loves New York. NO-ONE. And you know what else... YOU DON'T LIVE IN NEW YORK! SO TAKE OFF THE FUCKING I LOVE NY T-SHIRT!

I hate those people. The kind that wear a *Within Temptation* t-shirt because they like the logo but have never heard anything that isn't in the charts. The kind of twats that have a Brooklyn college hoodie despite the fact they've never been to college, or America. Pricks.

But anyway, as I was probably saying, tights suck.

But yeah, Joe, that's me. Don't ever call me Joey or I'll put you through a wall (literally, I have super powers). I live alone in a flat big enough that I could swing a cat, but small enough that I couldn't own the aforementioned cat. Which works out well because cats suck dick. Not literally of course (although there probably are people out there). But yeah, why would I want to own something that will at some point attack and scar me? I mean I've got a nemesis for that (but I'll tell you about him later). Right now I'm pissed off about cats. You feed them, look after them, spend money on them, and what do you get? Fuck all. I'd rather spend my money on a sex doll. At least that won't leave fur and shit all over the house (well, not unless I get really kinky).

Across the hall from my apartment lives a douche bag. I've never met him, not officially, but he's British. I sometimes hear him watching 'football' - that's enough for me. It's my understanding he supports a team called 'you reds' when they're winning and 'you bloody wankers' the rest of the time. I've never understood yelling at a sports match on the TV. I kind of get yelling if you're there in person. I mean, maybe they've forgotten to pass to that guy, or shoot, or not be a 'useless tosser', so I guess it's lucky these fans are there to help them out. But yelling at a TV? In my apartment building? That pisses me off.

Unfortunately as I can't reveal my identity or break the law by kicking his teeth in, there's not a lot I can do about it. One of the many downsides to being a superhero. I've seen a few superheroes have their identities revealed and it can get pretty dangerous (depending on how many people you've put behind bars, and how good they are at getting out again). I'm pretty sure the prison guards give them tools to get out on the sly, or maybe the 'Get out of jail free card' actually works? Or maybe it's just like religion: if you say you're sorry, they let you go.

Religion. Pfft! Don't even get me started.

So anyway, my building's not too bad. There's a nice old lady who sometimes takes in packages for me; sometimes even lets me have them back. And then of course there's Steve. Ah Steve. "Don't ever call me Steven or I'm leavin'" I should hate Steve, I really should. He's annoying, childish, a little bit racist at times, and most of all, he knows my secret identity. But for some reason I keep him around. Largely because he's reliable, but also he'd make a good human shield. Oh and he does make damn good lasagne. I did consider taking him on as a sidekick for a while, but when I listened to Rockman moan about Boulderkid for 3 hours without pausing for breath I decided maybe I was better as a lone super-wolf. It's all good having someone to back you up when you're out there, but Steve would probably be more BMX Bandit than Nightwing. Plus sidekicks grow up too fast these days, always sneaking off and getting in trouble. Nah, I like to keep my own time, fight crime when I want, not when I have to or my side kick dies, pah.

But yeah, Steve lives in the flat directly below me. On the night I discovered my super powers, I accidentally smashed through his ceiling. He was pretty nice about the whole thing; I got an old school mate in to fix it and paid for the whole thing. Steve didn't make much of a fuss, I think he was just excited to know a superhero. He even had a hand in designing my costume (although his idea of having my actual name stitched on the back like a football jersey wasn't one that made it past the design stage). I think he may be a bit special.

I do like my costume, tights excluded. It's simple, black and white, not too restrictive, tarantula emblem covering my face which makes me look badass. Although the first time I wore it out, I caught a quick glimpse of my mask in the reflection of a skyscraper, for some reason thought it was an actual spider and broke my own nose trying to squash it. You live and learn.

My weapon of choice: I carry The Stinger. It's basically a modified bat with a taser in the end. Unfortunately I wasn't blessed with the web slinging abilities of Spiderman, although I can walk up walls (if I ever run into Peter I must ask him what breed of spider bit him, because he clearly hit the jackpot). So yeah, I take bad guys down either with the taser end or with a firm whack to the head. Works pretty well I find.

Life as a super hero can be lonely so I'm glad for Steve. It gives me someone to talk to, even though it means I also have to listen (not really my strong point). Steve is some kind of IT worker for Norscorp I think. I've never really understood/given a shit what he does specifically, but as far as I can remember it involves replacing things that aren't the things that people want them to be? Like I said, I'm not a good listener, but he earns a decent wage, and it gets him away from me during the day.

'So are you going out on patrol tonight?' says Steve.

'Nah figure I'll save that for chapter 4', I reply.

'What's that now?'

'Oh nothing'.

Steve's over again, as you've probably guessed. He's had a bad day at work so I'm having to listen to him bitch like a little… well, bitch. I find it odd that the phrase 'Shut up Steve, no one cares about you or what you're saying' doesn't have the desired effect on this guy. He just laughs it off as if I'm joking. Luckily he's cooking dinner so I can only half hear him over the sizzling of the pan. Not sure what it'll be: looks like there's some kind of bolognaise in the pan I would guess. Could be chilli, heck, could be dog food. I don't have the most advanced taste palate: I like chips, I like pizza, I like burgers. The way I see it, it all gets processed in my belly, so if it's already processed, that'll make my stomach's job easier, right?

'So what do you think?' says Steve.

Shit. I was not expecting to be expected to have an opinion on this situation that I clearly haven't been listening to.

'Oh well, err...I say...go with your gut?' I stutter. 'Sky's the limit and all, don't be a lame... something, always take an... umbrella?'

'Hmm...yeah I suppose that's one way of looking at it', says Steve. 'You have such a unique take on the world Joe. I guess that's why I...'

Phew, dodged a bullet there. I know I said I don't give a shit, and that is true, but there's not giving a shit and then there's other people thinking you don't give a shit. Y'know? Maybe that doesn't make sense; as I said I mostly only talk to Steve these days. Well whatever, he's yammering on again, I should really listen to what he's saying. As I glance over to the TV there's a high speed chase happening on the news. They're calling for local superheroes to come help. This happens a lot, but there's so many superheroes these days I don't wanna cramp someone else's style. I slyly switch the channel; I know for a fact if Steve saw that he'd force me to go help out, and I haven't eaten yet. Plus I stopped that kid spray-painting yesterday. What do these people want from me? I can't be everywhere. I'm not a freaking super he... oh, scratch that, but I'm still not going. I haven't eaten, I might get cramp, or…

'Right, dinner, is, served', says Steve. 'I hope you don't mind, I made enchiladas.'

'I don't know what that is Steve', I reply. 'But good work. Let's get our grub on because I need to go fight some crime soon, meaning you'll have to go home.'

I think that's a polite way than telling him that if I have to listen to him whinge for much longer I'll fork myself in the eye. Plus there's a *Scrubs* marathon on in a bit and he talks over all the jokes.

CHAPTER THREE – (THE WEEKLY VISIT TO THE SIA)

So it's Friday which can only mean one thing: Kristine Appellio. Damn I wanna punch her in the jeans, both sexually and literally. Fridays in the superhero world are notorious for sucking balls, because Friday is check-in day. Which means reporting to your bitch of a handler, making a detailed report of any fights/arrests/incidents you may have been involved in, and of course the boring-as-shit presentation made by snooze-a-thon the 3rd or whatever his name is today. But at least that's just boring; this, this is torture.

'So, have you been keeping your profile up?' Kristine asks, with a sneering tone barely masking her contempt for me. I wouldn't mind, but it's not like I want to be here either.

'Yeah I've had a few run ins with some bad guys', I reply. 'Stopped a few robberies and such'.

The air is stale, I can almost hear her inner voices spitting venom.

'Oh, and I stopped a kid spray painting', I continue. 'Didn't have time to write that up, but I scared him straight'.

Scared him straight, scared him off, whatever. He definitely stopped what he was doing, at least until I left. I tell you, if it wasn't for that fine rack she has busting out of that loose top I'd probably say fuck it and not turn up at all. Of course then I'd be in a LOT more trouble; rogue superheroes are treated worse than the Supervillians these days. Well, except for Rogue, she's treated very well. But again, she's hot. Stupid double standards.

'And have you brought all your paperwork?' Kristine asks. 'Filled out, signed and dated?'

I hear her talking but it's difficult to concentrate. If I wasn't positive that she despised me in every way, I'd probably try to make a move. I guess she's seen it all before; superhero after superhero coming through here. There was a rumour that she was getting it on with Flashman a few months back. It certainly hasn't softened her demeanour in any way though. By the book, that's what she likes. On the book would be good, or next to it, bent over it... God damn it, what's she talking about?

'Is this literally all you've done this week?' she says.

Oh, she's reading my reports. Yeah they may be a bit sparse, but I've been busy. Bought myself one of those massaging chairs: those things take time.

'Err... Ahem! Yeah, well it's been a busy week', I say. 'Lots of recon and data... analysis? I think I'm getting close to finding The Dish's lair... I've heard a few things, got some leads and stuff...'

Oh yeah, The Dish is my current nemesis. We found each other through supersoftheworld.com. We seem to be pretty much polar opposites on all the big stuff: he wants to destroy the world, I'd quite like him not to; he thinks people are scum, I mask that opinion so as not to cause offence. He thought the film version of *Hitchhikers Guide to the Galaxy* wasn't a pile of shit. Like I said, polar opposites on all the big stuff, but mostly he also seemed a bit lazy and didn't like to work weekends so it seemed a good fit. Low-maintenance bad guy. He's been pretty good for me, although the constant puns get a bit much. Oh, surprise surprise it looks like old Miss Angrypants Appellio is screaming again, I should probably take note...

'We expect a certain amount of results from you superheroes', Kristine screams. 'We have targets, quotas that need meeting, and you, Arachno, are not helping with these, what... two arrests? One of them was for JAYWALKING? Why can't you be more like Flashman? He does wonders for this office.'

Well yeah, but he has x-ray vision, super speed and a sidekick who can predict the future. How am I supposed to compete with that? Plus he's doinking little Ms Appellio. I bet that improves his standing, lying down, bending, I bet she's proper kinky...

'I have superiors to answer to and your leads and whispers are not what they want,' she continues. 'Now either catch your nemesis soon or find a medium-level crook and take him down. I don't want another week of petty crap that regular police officers could take care of. We pay you a rather handsome amount of money to be a superhero, so go and be a super-fricking-hero.'

She'll get over it, all that grunting and yelling... Maybe she does want me. I've never been good at reading women. Punching bad guys, easy. Disarming super lasers, no problem. Saying the right thing to a beautiful girl, impossible. I'd rather diffuse an atomic bomb. At least when that explodes in your face it'll kill you.

Ah well, time for the seminar of boring, I guess. I wonder who'll be making a presentation today. I did enjoy the one a few weeks ago about what to do if you get shrunk and stuck in the ear of a ferret; strangely specific and not very useful, but some of the slides the guy used had me in stitches. The presentation on infected stitches on the other hand... yuck. Remind me never to - what was it? - use any old syringe you find on the street as a makeshift needle? Seriously, who would do that? Ew.

I guess some superheroes are stupid. Like, really stupid. I met a superhero once whose power was being able to answer questions in 40 different languages, but didn't have the power to understand what he was saying. There are some oddballs out there. Captain Oddballs for one (I'm still not sure when the ability to inflate your testicles is helpful, but he seemed rather proud of himself so I didn't press the matter). Ah here we are, a 45 minute presentation on... huh? The 10 differences between regular breasts and superwomen breasts? You know what? I may pay attention to this one.

CHAPTER 4 – (OUT ON PATROL)

Patrol. Some people love this part of the job; me, I find it kind of boring. I mean sure you come across petty criminals and build up your arrest report, which appeases Kirstine Appellitits. You can walk the streets, lose yourself for a bit. My favourite (well, only enjoyable) part is scouting out St Claire street, and that's because of Louise. At least that's what I've called her; never had the balls to actually talk to her to find out but she looks like a Louise. Gorgeous blonde curly locks falling over her beautiful little face, the sort of eyes that say come get me, the sort of mouth that says come kiss me, and the sort of tits that say come on me... that was crude, I apologise.

But seriously, seeing her makes my day. She works at Double Down Donuts, serving coffee to losers. She served me some coffee once. I really hate coffee but I thought it'd be a good opener.

It wasn't.

I'd planned it all out, word for word: she'd pour me a coffee, I'd say 'Actually I don't like black coffee, but I do like you, wanna go on a date?' Kind of smooth right? Well, for me anyway. But it all went to shit. I went in, asked for a coffee, in my head saying over and over again 'I don't like black coffee, I don't like black coffee', not listening to anything around me. Which is where I went wrong. As she brought over my coffee she was saying to her friend 'I don't see why people are so racist, I mean as far as I'm concerned all people are born the same, am I right mister?' to which I turned around and blurted out in a surprisingly loud and petrified voice 'Actually, I don't like black'.

Dead silence as everyone in the room stared at me. 'Coffee', I added, desperately. 'I meant to say black *coffee*. You're not black, err wanna go on a... oh god... I'm not a... I, oh shit. Excuse me.'

I walked out of there and haven't had the balls to go back. There's not many ways of making a worse first impression. Something about the phrase 'I'm not racist' always make people seem racist. Maybe that's because it's usually followed by a 'but' which in my experience is then followed by an incredibly racist and offensive opinion. It's a bit like saying 'I'm not going to pull your pants over your head and call you a ferret tickler', as you reach for their waistband. I don't like those kinds of people.

Anyway, since I can't unlive that incident I just sit on top of the roof opposite and watch her work. She really is amazing: constantly smiling, always on the ball, God she's perfect. If I could just convince her I'm not racist. Which I'm not... See? Now you think maybe I secretly am, don't you? Sometimes I hope that a black guy will get mugged outside her coffee shop and I can swoop down in front of her and save the day, or get in the paper for setting up some kind of anti-racist rally? But I don't have the effort for that level of organisation so I just sit, and watch, like a stalker. I wish one of my superpowers would've been the ability to not make an ass out of myself around women.

I texted The Dish earlier just to check he's not up to anything dastardly that I should know about. He said he's halfway through the third season of Breaking Bad, but after the next episode has finished he's going to get on with his death ray. He's been saying that for weeks. It's one of my favourite things about The Dish: he has almost no motivation. I think in the three years I've been a superhero we've had three battles.

The first was completely on the rooftops. He'd made a giant fly swatter that was supposed to crush me. I did explain I was a spider, but he said he'd put a lot of effort into it, so I let it go. We fought for about an hour and a half, with an agreed break of ten minutes in the middle as I'd forgotten to hang my washing out. It was ok. Physically we're quite evenly matched so it was pretty intense, but he managed to escape 'unfortunately'. He texted me later that night asking if we could do it in a more public location next time because he felt all his dish-based puns were wasted. I was the only one who could hear them, although I think his best one that night was 'you better throw in the tea towel' which is pretty poor. I told him that if he spent some time coming up with a higher level of pun then I'd be happy to increase the number of bystanders, I mean the publicity certainly wouldn't do me any harm.

And so the second battle was in a pub called *Bendies*. Not as nice a place as it sounds, and it did not go as planned for either of us. Basically we'd agreed to meet there at around 9pm, which I said was a bit late but I figured I could get a drink in first. And so at 9pm The Dish bursts through the door and yells 'Arachno! Looks like you're all washed up, time to come clean!' which made everyone in the bar groan, even the ones who weren't aware of who he was (although the helmet in the shape of a dish - which he insists looks cool, despite the floral pattern running round the edge which makes his head look a bit like a flower - and the yellow and green shoulder/scouring pads were probably an indication). He ran at me, with his marigolds clutching what looked like a dildo, but I later found out was some kind of baton covered in bristles which he'd named 'the scrubber'. I stood up ready for the oncoming onslaught and just as he was about to land the first blow the barman grabbed him by the scruff of his neck and walked him outside. I was then politely asked to leave. 'This isn't one of those pubs thank you very much,' said the barman, and that was that. We both decided to grab a donut and had quite a nice chat. We decided that bars were not the place for an ultimate showdown between good and evil, so we called it a night. I watched a few episodes of Castle and drifted off to sleep, mildly annoyed at myself, and at The Dish.

The third time we met was a properly awesome battle. He'd made himself a big old suit that shot fire, and made him 10 times stronger. It was pretty awesome but I was annoyed it didn't seem to have anything to do with his moniker. He justified it by saying he'd 'used everything but the kitchen sink to build it'. I called him lame, but the fight was on. We'd picked a nice spot: it was a park so there were a lot of families and such around, although it was such a large space that it was unlikely anyone would get hurt, which I was happy with. I've seen the forms you have to fill out for when you hurt a civilian, and they are long and boring. Fuck that. But he was still a threat to the public, technically, so if I could arrest him this was going to look good. I did kind of wish there were more buildings around for me to show off my wall climbing abilities as parks don't present a lot of wall climbing opportunities. But I still had my stinger, recently painted black with red go-faster stripes down the side, y'know, so I could twat crime faster. Yeah that's right.

Anyway, we actually had good fight. Pretty standard hero vs villain bout. We made sure that if either of us had a quip we'd move closer to the onlookers so that they could hear it and hopefully make a note for the papers. I spent most of the previous night trying to come up with some good ones. I wanted to say something about Greeks and smashing plates, and stuff, but I couldn't quite get the wording right. Plus there was a *Happy Endings* marathon on so I was quite distracted. I did come up with 'You look rather dish-evilled'. Nice right? And I seem to remember saying something along the lines of, 'You better switch to cable because I'm going to break your face'. Yeah that one didn't quite come out right. In the end the only line that made the papers was 'I guess my arachno-foe be ya'. I regretted saying it the instant it came out of my mouth, but yeah, that's now in black and white, framed, on my mother's wall forever.

I managed to disable his super suit by randomly pulling wires out of the back. I didn't really pay attention in college but I figured one of them was probably essential and I was right; he powered down, cursed, and then fell out of the suit. My first victory! Of course as I went to handcuff him, to take him into custody he, apparently accidentally, tripped and set off a smoke grenade. By the time I'd finished coughing up a lung he was gone, which was good because I would've had to find myself a new arch nemesis if he was in jail, which I was not really up for. But as soon as his death ray is finished, my God we'll have a showdown, just you wait and see.

CHAPTER 5 – (BACK ON PATROL AGAIN)

'All I'm saying is it'd be good for your profile.'

Here we go again, Steve banging on and on about forming a super group.

'You'd get to hang out with other superheroes,' he continued. 'Take on different bad guys, you may even have fun. Make some new friends, learn about yourself. You could be the next *Avengers* or *Justice League*.'

'Well yeah Steve,' I reply. 'Except I don't really care about justice and I have nothing to avenge. I'm not even sure those guys do. It's not a great name really. I'd have called them *The Protectors*, or *The Over-inflated Egos*, but that's just me.'

'Well exactly! You could be the one to form *The Protectors*, or the over infiltrated whatsits.'

Bless him. As much as I appreciate the company of Steve it does pain me that he's such a fucking idiot. I told him once that a cockroach I found in my apartment was Antman. He must've spent three hours asking that thing questions about Tony Stark, and boy, his face when I squashed it, he nearly had a heart attack. But yeah, while he drives me a little mad, he also keeps me sane, which is why I've let him tag along on patrol tonight. I've picked a quiet part of town; I doubt we'll run into any trouble. Sometimes it's nice to get out the apartment for a bit.

'You could call yourselves the insect-urity patrol,' Steve persisted. 'Y'know if you found more insect-based superheroes...'

Give me strength. I mean, don't get me wrong, having some kind of group of superheroes is cool, plus it relieves the pressure of catching criminals if the others are doing it for you. Then there's the tax breaks...

'The POW-er rangers?'

I have the strength to literally squeeze his face until it pops... I wonder if anyone would miss him...

'What about the *Superheroes Taking on Every Villian on Earth*!'

'Why on earth would we call ourselves that?' I reply.

'Well that's kind of what you guys do isn't it? Plus it spells out STEVE, which would be frickin awesome. You'd be all like – I'm just gonna head out with STEVE to fight crime and patrol the city!'

'That's literally what I'm doing. I mean right this second, what you've just described is the thing that's happening.'

'Yeah but in that scenario, I'm not Steve. STEVE is Steve, and they're all super people. Y'see?'

This could be a long night.

'Okay, but if the team is called STEVE,' I say, 'surely I wouldn't say I'm going out with STEVE, because I'm part of STEVE?'

'Hmm... I see your point. Okay back to the drawing board. Hey, what about *The Drawing Board*?'

I could just crush his trachea until the noise stopped. If I was ever held up in a court of law I could plead that he was being fuckin' annoying, anyone who's ever met him could vouch for that. Huh, here's some trouble...

'Steve, wait here,' I say. 'I'm gonna go investigate those shady looking guys'.

It's probably nothing, but it's late, they're wearing dark trench coats and loading something into a van that looks a tad suspicious...

'Good evening cuntflappers', I say. Really must remember to work on my opening line, I use 'cuntflappers' far too often.

'Well looky here, looks like we've got ourselves a spider, man', says one of the guys.

Very original. Prick. 'I... am Arachno, and you'd do well to watch your tone young man!'

'Iraq no? You some kind of racist against Muslims or something?'

'No, not "Iraq no", ARACHNO! ... like a spider?'

'You mean like Spiderma...'

'No! Not like him. I'm much better, I am...'

'Can you walk up walls?'

'Yeah.'

'Can you shoot webs?'

'Well... no... but...'

'Spiderman can shoot webs.'

'Yes, I'm well aware of what he can do.'

'Are you two friends?'

'What? Well, no we're not friends...' *Although if he ever accepts my Facebook friend request I could pass him off as a friend...*

'Well anyway Flymo, what the hell are you bothering us for?'

'ARACHO! And... I dunno. You just seemed a bit shifty... are you a bit shifty?'

'Not especially, I don't think.'

'Well what are you doing down this dark alley so late at night loading stuff?'

'Well... We're loading stuff? That our job y'see.'

Ah crap, legitimate workers? This has got awkward pretty quick. 'Is anything that you're doing illegal at all?'

'Nope.'

'A bit dodgy?'

'Nope.'

'Underhanded at least?'

'Nope. We are loading stuff, on to this van, then going to bed'.

Balls. 'Well... carry on citizens. The ever-watchful eye of justice is lurking'.

'Is that yours?'

'Is what mine?'

'The ever-watchful eye? Is it your eye?'

'Well, yes.'

'Huh. Makes you sound like a bit of a perv if you ask me...'

As he wanders off towards his van I'm thinking he probably had a point. That did sound a bit weird, not really sure where it came from. Oh well, better get back to Steve.

'What happened there?' says Steve.

'False alarm,' I reply.

'Fair enough. How about *The Eight Leg Gang*?'

I need some new friends...

CHAPTER 6 – (A PROBLEM ARRIVES)

Urgh. Two o'clock already and still not a wink of sleep, it's my own fault: that sixth beer was not necessary. I tried counting sheep to send me off to sleep, but I came up with a better system where I group them together to make it quicker and easier to count. In case you ever decide to try it, there are 178. You're welcome. Not sure how that knowledge is meant to help anyone sleep, maybe I'm doing it wrong. Is that a knocking on my door? Pretty faint, but my senses are heightened compared to regular people. It gets annoying at the cinema, or in libraries, or at orgies. There it is again, but louder. I'm pretty sure there's someone out there, I should go take a look...

'Psst! Aracho!' says a voice by the door. 'Are you in? Open up. Quick.'

Hmm... well this doesn't sound good. There are only three people who know my identity and where I live. Steve, who only refers to me as Joe, or Champ, or sometimes 'my buddy with a secret' although I've asked him not to call me that in front of people (it gives off a very strange vibe). Kristine Appellio, I'm pretty sure would never talk to me outside of work let alone come to my house at two in the morning. Which means it must be, oh god no... not him....

'Open up dude, I'm in trouble,' says the voice.

Well this is no surprise. 'What do you want Flame-buoyant?' I reply.

I'd first met Flame-buoyant at a party after a particularly boring training day. He seemed like a nice guy, bit over zealous, slightly egocentric, but he seemed harmless. We had a few shots, exchanged a few stories. We were both new to the superhero game so they weren't the most exciting stories, but with every shot, our stories got bigger, more impressive, more made up and more slurred, until we could barely sit up straight.

And so what with me only living round the corner he crashed on my sofa, breaking one of the 13 rules of the SIA. The next morning, feeling a little worse for wear, we grabbed a breakfast from the diner across the street and then went our separate ways. We've run into each other once or twice throughout the years, occasionally stopping to swap stories, have a catch up, the usual. Last I heard he kept accidentally setting fire to things. Seems his fire ability is harder to control the more angry he gets, and what with his job being in the DMV and therefore mostly involving being yelled at quite a lot about things he wasn't responsible for, every day is a struggle. I often remarked he should've just become a super villain; the job would've suited him better, but his mother had convinced him that heroism was the way forward, maybe he'd meet a nice girl and settle down and blah blah blah. Fuckin' mothers eh?

'Just let me in dude', he persisted. 'I'll explain. Just, y'know, not through a door.'

I'm always nervous of opening my door at night, even being a superhero. I mean, what if there's a weirdo out there? Or a psycho? Or even worse a Jehovah's Witness? It doesn't bear thinking about. But against my better judgement, I let the fucker in.

'Thanks dude,' he said.

'Woah what happened to your face?'

'It is a long story. You got any Scotch?'

And so he sat down and told me exactly what happened. It was, as he had said, a long story. But I'll give you the short version because you've got things to do...

Flame-buoyant had been working the lower east-side. The crime rate there is crazy high, thus my being on the upper west-side. I'm not an idiot. But he loves it because he can pick off the easier-to-catch criminals and it makes his arrests file look better than it actually is. It's a nice plan but it involves stuff and things, neither of which appeal to me. I got a good thing going.

But I digress... so he took down this villain 'Miss Tletoe'. I think she liked guys going under her and kissing? I don't know or care. Anyway, to try and get out of it she'd offered up some info on The Vapour, one of the most notorious supervillains there is. High-level superheroes have been after him for years but he always manages to get away, so obviously Flamey, as I don't like to call him, jumped at the opportunity to take down such a massive target. She gave him details of where he'd be and when, so he let her go and headed straight there.

Of course what she failed to mention was that he was actually negotiating with the police chief his terms of surrender. For some reason The Vapour had turned over a new leaf. Maybe he found God. Maybe he realised God was clearly an outdated idea and grew up. Either way he had decided to give himself up but with a reduced sentence for ratting out his fellow scum. Bit of a scummy move, but you'd expect that from scum. But Flame-buoyant, none the wiser to the situation, burst in, to everyone's surprise, promptly alerting both The Vapour's henchmen and the Police Chief's security, at which point they all opened fire in every direction. Long and the short of it, most people in the room wound up dead and the ones that didn't (e.g. the Police Chief) were pissed. Which brings us up to date.

'So... basically, you're responsible for killing a lot of people?' I say.

'Well... no... I just happened to trigger an event that ended in lots of dead people.'

'Including The Vapour?'

'Yeah, and a lot of his henchmen.'

'Well that's probably a good thing...'

'...and quite a few police officers.'

'That is the opposite of a good thing. So, knowing that all this has happened, why in the blue hell would you come to me?'

'Because you're my only hope Obi-Wan.'

'...'

'Star Wars?'

'...'

'Really? Ok well, you are the only person who can help.'

This guy is screwed.

CHAPTER SEVEN – (A GLIMPSE INSIDE THE HEAD OF THE DISH)

I am the holder of your food. I wait, silently, sometimes on my side, in a rack. You will wash me without thought. I can smash without mercy. I am... The Dish.

But you can call me Phil. Both my friends do. Life as a supervillain is hard. You really have to balance your work life and your home life as they can get pretty similar. Especially if you can only cover the rent on one place. I'm currently living in my secret base of evil. It's only got a microwave, which is a problem because pot noodles, whilst tasting like shit, are, well, they're not the healthy choice I promised mum I'd make when I moved to the big city.

Ah the big city. It's quite different from where I grew up. My village was so boring I had names for the squirrels. But enough about ball, bag and bender; we're talking about me, The Dish. Extraordinary supervillain. My muscles make men cower, my puns have people wanting to throw in the tea towel. Do you like that? I just made that up off the top of my head. I'm very, very clever.

Throughout my many scrapes through the years one of my greatest foes has been Arachno. He has somehow bested me on every occasion so far, which gets me a little bit miffed. Luckily, due to my amazing skill, foresight and dastardliness I have always managed to slip through his fingers. Did mention I'm amazing? Or was that you? Yeah it was probably you saying how gorgeous I am. They call me The Dish because I was told from a very young age that I was incredibly handsome; both my mother and my aunt agree I'm possibly the most beautiful thing in the world and I can't think of a reason they would lie.

My father was a businessman. We'd only see him on weekends, but he always came home smelling of success and what I now know to be the smell of other women. Retrospectively, he was a bit of a dick, but back then I idolised him. When no one was around I'd put on his gigantic suit jacket and yell at my toys the same way he did on the phone every now and then. It felt good, much better than mum's stockings.

So you're probably wondering why I became a supervillain, or you're just wondering how did I get this damn good looking? I tell you, this overbite didn't happen on its own, and if it weren't for years of acne my face wouldn't be so uniquely bumpy, plus my thick prescription glasses really emphasise how sexy my eyes are when I'm squinting. Hey. Some guys are just lucky, you are welcome. But if you can get over my rugged good looks, you'll notice the tortured soul behind chiselled perfection.

I was teased as a boy, mostly due to the fact my Adidas tracksuit had an extra stripe (my mum couldn't afford the Tippex Mouse like the other kids' mums). Oh and I had a very pronounced lisp. At first the bullying didn't bother me, but then it did and that brings us up to date.

Oh I forgot to mention, my dad's a crimelord. He took me on as an apprentice when I turned sixteen; at seventeen he kicked me out and told me not to come back until I was a real villain. Like I said, dick.

So I started with some petty crime. Y'know, hustling, pick pocketing, grand larceny, but nothing seemed to impress big ol' dad. Then one day a flyer came through my letter box: *become a super villain and spend your life chillin.*

Don't get me wrong, leaflets in general make me angry. I mean, if I want a pizza I'll go to the nearest pizza shop, not the one that's posted so many leaflets through my door I can no longer get out my house. But this leaflet was different. It wasn't asking me to sell my house, it wasn't inviting me to switch banks, it was telling me I could have a job and still do nothing. I mean, that's the dream right?

So I gave them a call, gave them most of my savings, and they gave me just enough pointers that I didn't feel ripped off. They have meetings once a week which technically I'm allowed to go to now I'm part of the SIA, but jeez are they boring. It's mostly villains moaning about being thwarted. Being thwarted never bothered me, it's part of the package. I mean, if every supervillain's plans worked we'd have a new world ruler every other day. I mean what's the point? I'd rather try every now and then, fail, grab a Dominoes, kick back and watch some re-runs of *30 Rock*. One day I'll take over the world (no I won't), one day...

CHAPTER EIGHT – (BACK TO THE FLAMING PROBLEM)

'Ok Flamey Boy-Ant', I say. 'What's the deal? What do you need and, most importantly, how do I make you go away?'

'I need help, Arachno', he replies. 'They're going to lock me up for this, for a long time. I totally ruined everyone's plans, got a bunch of people killed, and blew a deal that would have seen half the criminals in this town in jail before the end of the day.'

'Still failing to see what this has to do with me...?'

'Well... didn't you once talk about a time-travelling girl...?

Shit. This is the problem with drinking and talking: you do a bit too much of one, you do a bit too much of the other. It's true, I had told him about this girl. I guess I neglected to mention *how* I 'knew' her.

Basically, she dated The Dish for a few months. I'd found out about her from Steve doing some recon for me. I was going to do it myself but I had cramp or something more believable. Whatever, he likes doing it so shut up. Apparently she could jump back in time, but only a few hours – still quite impressive. Apparently she mostly used to it go back in time before an argument just so she could be doubly as pissed and come up with better comebacks. I think that's unfair: women are already so good at arguing.

Needless to say, the constant losing of arguments got too much for The Dish and he chucked her, eventually. It made for an awkward and out of place quip I threw at him the following week during a battle for which I apologised, and later berated Steve for not letting me know they'd split up. I mean there's no fun in being a dick. But anyway, I knew what Flame-buoyant was going to ask and I couldn't think of a way to say no. The Dish is NOT going to be happy...

'Ok, I guess I can ask', I say. 'But I'm making no promises.'

'Oh come on,' Flame-buoyant replies. 'After the way you rocked her world so hard she went back in time just so you could rock her again?'

I may have slightly twisted the facts when telling this story.

'Let me make a phone call.'

This is going to be awkward.

CHAPTER NINE – (BACK INSIDE THE DISH'S HEAD)

My god Malcolm Reynolds is cool. I wish I could be a space cowboy.

The phone's ringing, oh shit, why is my phone ringing. It can't be Mum, I phoned her a few weeks ago. God why are parents so needy? Just give me your money and leave me alone for Christ's sake. It's like they think I owe them something. Where is it? Should really have a clean up around here. Ah there it is... Arachno... hmm... this can't be good. He usually texts about the death ray or general smack talk... Just quickly check the internet... no new spoilers for the new Avengers movie... I have a very, very bad feeling about this...

'Mmmmyellow?' I say.

'Hi... Dish...' the voice on the other end says.

'It's *The* Dish.'

'Right, sorry, yeah of course, it's Arachno. Y'know, arch-nemesis guy?'

'Yes, I am aware of you. Why are you calling me? We're not scheduled for a public confrontation 'til... next... Wednesday according to my diary. Has something come up? Was I supposed to be somewhere? I haven't received any emails.'

'No it's not that, it's... do you remember Jean Strumper the time jumper?'

Do I remember Jean Strumper the time jumper? What kind of a question is that? You stole the only girl I ever loved, causing me to completely lose my mind and turn evil... Okay that's not true, but I think it would've made a better backstory for me. Maybe I'll get retconned later or something? That'd be a sweet backstory. Ah Jean, she was crazy hot. Emphasis on the crazy: that girl was like a minefield of crazy. The littlest things would set her off, plus she always had the best comebacks. It wasn't fair. Then again she did used to clean the dishes pretty well, if you catch my drift. Man, I haven't thought about her in a while. I should really call her.

'Well I was wondering,' continues Arachno. 'If you could, maybe, call her?'

'Definitely not,' I reply. 'That's a terrible idea.'

Curse you foolish pride. Always listen to my gut reaction, that's how I ended up with a pair of Dre Beats headphones sitting in a cupboard gaining more dust than a vacuum cleaner. Although, if he's got a reason to call her that would be a nice opener. Maybe I could sneak my way back into her, life.

'Please mate, I've got a major situation that I kind of need sorted.'

If that situation is in his pants then so help me God.

'We just need to use her powers,' Arachno continues. 'I need to jump back a few hours, but it's got to happen now.'

Hmm... it's always good to have your arch nemesis in your debt. Maybe he'll go easy on me, make me look better in front of the public, or let me get away when I trip over my cape again...

'I don't think I can help,' I reply. 'I've not spoken to Jean in a long time and we didn't exactly part on good terms.'

'Please Dish, just give me her number. I'll sort it out.'

'No no, I should be the one to talk to her. I mean, she doesn't know who you are right?'

'Huh. Yeah I hadn't thought of that. Ok well can you set up a meeting, say, one hour, Walmart car park?'

'I'll see what I can do…'

'Ok, you're not going to use this as an excuse to get back in her pants? You guys were NOT good for each other at all.'

'Oh come on, have some faith in me. I'm merely doing you a favour'

Of course it wouldn't hurt seeing her again.

CHAPTER TEN – (OUR BRAVE HERO COMES FACE TO FACE WITH THE DISH AND HIS EX)

I got a text from The Dish saying it was all set up and that he'd see me there. I wasn't sure why he wanted to be there so bad but I had my suspicions that it involved his penis. Although that wasn't my issue. My issue was to solve this problem with Flamey before it became my problem. Harbouring a fugitive I'm pretty sure is a bad thing, and while I've not been near any water I'm pretty sure what I'm doing still counts as bad.

So here we are, perched on the wall behind Walmart. I wasn't sure what the correct etiquette was so I suited up anyway. Flame-buoyant's armbands, much like his body, were deflated so he looked like a used-up sex doll. I was always confused by his superhero name. I mean, buoyancy has never been linked to flames, and seeing as his power didn't seem to have anything to do with water it made the luminous yellow swimming goggles, armbands and lifebelt more confusing than anything else. I'm guessing when he got to the front of the registration desk queue 'Flame-boy' was already taken and he panicked.

'Do you think she'll come?' he says.

'Do you think I can see the future?' I reply. 'Shut up Flame-face. The Dish said she'd come, so she'll come.'

Urgh. I hate waiting. Waiting and talking to dickheads are like my two least favourite things to do and yet here I am. There's a rustling over in the bushes; could be her, could be a rat, could be a pervert... oh, it's The Dish, I guess I was almost right. I pretend I haven't seen him, it's quite clear he's come up with a big entrance so I'll let him have his moment.

'So when the chips are down', says The Dish. 'You need a Dish to put them on'.

'Really...?' I reply.

'What? It kind of works...'

'I thought it was nice', says Flame-buoyant. 'He's combined the two uses of the word chips to make a clever pun involving his name and the situation. He's like that late night host guy who does the jokes.'

'Shut up Lame-boy, no one's talking to you', I reply. 'So she's coming?'

'Oh yes, she is most definitely coming,' Dish says, a little too enthusiastically. 'I sent out a message from my satellite Dish!'

'You know, not everything you say has to be a pun,' I mumble.

Sometimes I wish for a less talkative adversary. 'Hulk smash', 'I am Groot', that kind of thing. The only thing more embarrassing than a bad pun is a bad pun delivered by a man in Spandex. Luckily at that point a beautiful girl, dressed in a full-leather catsuit appears in front of us. The kind of girl you know could break you in an instant and you'd definitely let her.

'So, now that that's sorted shall we begin?' she says.

'Strange opener?' I blurt out.

'Oh I'm sorry, let me catch you up. I got here, you explained the situation, Dish drooled over me and pleaded for me to take him back, which was super pathetic FYI. You made several vaguely amusing references to my boobs and this guy ate a Mars Bar. Riveting stuff. It's a shame you'll have to miss it. Anyway, you agreed to give me 500 dollars and a signed picture which I said I didn't want, then I travelled back in time to save you the effort of all that. Also we're on a clock here if you want to get back before this idiot ruins everything. Are we ready?'

I hate time travellers. Always so fucking smug. Although it was a fair point, we didn't have much time given she can only go back a few hours. The longer we left it the less chance she could jump back far enough. Plus she had some lovely mammaries going on so I felt we could trust her. I wonder what references I made...

'Everyone grab hold of me,' she says.

Dish grabbed her hand, Flame grabbed the other, it seemed only fair that I got a boob. There was a flash of light...

CHAPTER ELEVEN – (BACK IN TIME)

So here we are, back earlier that night. Seems a bit rubbish: I always assumed if I went back in time I'd go to World War Two and punch Hitler in the knackers, or medieval times to see King Arthur and all that shit. Going back in time to just before I'd eaten seemed a bit of a letdown. Plus I'm hungry again now.

'Now unfortunately I cannot move in space only time', says Jean. 'And so we need to locate where you are and stop you from going to that meeting. Do you know – Dish stop staring at me – do you know where you are at the moment?'

'Ok, it's 22:20 so I'd be over on the embankment,' says Flame-buoyant. 'Possibly apprehending Miss Tletoe.'

'Miss Tletoe is a terrible name,' says Jean.

'Well that's just rude,' I say. 'I mean your name's only good because it rhymes, what if, instead of being a time jumper, you could breathe fire? Then you'd be Jean Strumper the fire breather, which is shit. So shut up and let's get moving.'

That was probably a bit harsh, but I've got things to do. I wonder if I've still watched the last episode of *Bones* in this time line. Time travel makes my head hurt.

We head to the embankment where Flame reckoned he was. He wasn't there. Turns out Flamey, as well as being a grade-A dickhead, also isn't a good time keeper. And so we retrace his steps as best he can remember until we find Miss Tletoe.

'Hey Miss, have you seen this guy?' I say, pointing at Flame.

Probably a slightly confusing opener now I think about it.

'I mean, not this guy, I mean, *the other* this guy?'

Yep, that straightened that one out.

Luckily Jean is a bit more proactive and forthcoming. And did I mention smoking hot? I should probably stop fixating on that. I was gazing at her bum when I realised she had Miss Tletoe against the wall trying to make her talk, which was nice because it meant I could stare at her bum. God bless the guy who made leather. And also, if anyone can make this girl talk, it's Jean and those sweater puppies of hers.

The other thing that's worth pointing out is Miss Tletoe's power is being able to make anyone kiss her. So me, Dish and Flamey were super-excited to see them hash it out. You don't often see lesbian superheroes, I wonder why that is. Surely it's what everyone wants? I mean there's the gay dudes in *Young Avengers* and all, but lesbians are pretty thin on the ground. Plus they're pretty on the ground... if they're thin. I don't wanna see two fatties going at it: that does nothing for me. There should only be four things wobbling in a lesbian wrestle and that does not include chins, bingo wings or bellies. Yuck. But anyway, I digress, and fighting crime with a boner is not easy/acceptable, apparently. Huh, looks like Miss Tletoe's out and we have our info. Awesome.

'Where did you learn to do that then?' I say

'Err... it's like superhero 102', says Jean 'Do you not go to the lectures?'

'I go to some of them... but I've got things to do. Y'know, all that crime fighting, plus *Game of Thrones* and things.'

'Oh man, I LOVE *Game of Thrones*. I was so happy when Joffrey kicked it. So who's your case worker?'

This girl is all kinds of awesome.

'Err... Kristine Appellio?'

'No way? She's mine too. Isn't she just the worst? I mean, don't get me wrong, she's hot and all, and banging most guys from what I hear. But she is just such a moaning bitch right?'

I think I may have to marry this girl. So once Miss Tletoe (Jean's right it is a stupid name) spilled the beans about what was going down, where and why, we headed in the direction that she pointed us and within a few minutes we were approaching the hideout where the deal was going down.

'Yeah, I remember this place', says Flame-buoyant. 'I crept up that flight of stairs and burst through that door, and then all hell opened up. Bang bang bang! Gun shots.'

I'm glad he cleared that up, I'd hate to burst into a massive orgy. We ran towards the door to stop the previous version of Flame but he was nowhere to be found. We peered through the window just in time to see him burst through the door on the other side of the building.

'Oh. Yeah maybe it wasn't this door...' Flame says.

'God damn you're an idiot,' I say. 'I mean seriously, how can you not remember what happened TODAY?'

Jean let out a scream of frustration. Understandable, but alerting all the men with guns to our whereabouts. Luckily she's a time traveller so we all grabbed her and jumped back ten minutes.

'Ok, let's walk around to the right door this time, yes?' says Dish.

'Good plan, I like this girl,' says Flame. 'Why did you let her go, Dish?

'Shut up, Flame, or I will Dish out some pain on your face.'

Dish had been useless and mostly sulking since we got here, probably because his plan to get back with Jean had failed in a time line that technically didn't even happen. I mean that's got to suck. We made our way round the building trying to avoid the security/mob until we arrived at the other door as past-Flame arrived. Flame stepped forward.

'Hey you,' he says.

'Me?' past Flame replies.

'Yes me.'

'You?'

Hmm...

'Ok can someone who isn't an idiot talk to him?'

I pull him to one side. 'Hey Flame, remember me?' I say.

'Sure Joe, how's it going?'

'Joe?' says Jean.

'Shut up, Jean, you didn't hear that,' I say. 'Now, we've come back, with you – see, that's you over there, wave Flame, good. We've come back to stop you from going in there.'

'But I am the defender of the people,' says past-Flame. 'The floating flame in the sea of darkness.'

That's actually quite a nice line, and almost justifies his ridiculous name. Almost.

'Yeah well if you go in there everyone dies and you go to jail. So walk away, go find someone else to arrest ok? Just do not enter that door. Tell him Flame.'

'Yeah sorry Me. I kind of messed up', says Flame. 'Got a bit too big for my boots, a bit too huge for my hubris, a bit too large for my...'

'Yes, well, I think we've had quite enough of that for one day, now go on, run along...'

I was about to turn around to ask Jean about alternate timelines and all that back to the future shit, but as I turned I saw our version of Flame disappear into nothing. Timeline correcting itself I guess. If only both of them had disappeared...

'Shall we go home then?' I say.

'Yeah no problem,' says Jean. '...Don't grab my tit this time.'

As I begrudgingly grab her hand there's a flash of light again and we appear back in our present time just in time to see the police and The Vapour leaving. The Vapour in cuffs and not a dead guy in sight.

'Well that seemed to work out alright,' I say.

'Yes it did, now, where's my money?' says Jean.

'Ah of course of course, I'll have to stop at an ATM. Then later I'll go beat it out of Flamey. Say, is he going to remember agreeing to this deal? Stupid time travel. You wanna go grab a drink on the way?'

'Yeah ok, where do you fancy?'

'Well, there's a lovely coffee shop on St Claire's Street I've been meaning to try. See you later Dish, and thanks for helping out.'

I could be wrong but there seems to be a quiet fury in his eye and yet also a wry smile as I walk off arm in arm with his former girlfriend. Not sure what that's all about but hey ho. I can't see him minding, I mean, it won't be a problem right? Right? Why are you looking at me like that?

CHAPTER TWELVE – (AND SO ENTER THE JURY)

So me and Jean are walking towards the cafe, just about to finally step into the lions mouth, bite the bullet, take the plunge, enter the... wow literally all my metaphors sound like vague innuendo today... All of a sudden a massive bright white light surrounds us, as my vision slowly returns I can make out twelve blobs around us, all wearing black cloaks, no wait not blobs... worse than blobs... oh no, teenagers!

'Arachno! The Jury finds you GUILTY!'

A timid, cracking voice says behind me I have heard rumours of these guys, bunch of little punks running around, thinking they're somehow above the law, if anyone's going to be above the law it really should be me – imagine if I was above the law, all the things I could do, I mean, I can't think of any right now... maybe I could take someone's boat. Wow. That is a shit idea, I am really not on the ball today.

'Hey Jean, would you mind taking us back in time, before these little bitches jumped us, even better before these guys balls dropped... so three or four minutes?' I give a wry smile at my smooth bit of candour, goddamn I bet she thinks I'm cool... she's unconscious.

'Oh come on guys! I was quipping! Quipping!' I say, frustrated at the wasted energy.

One of the spotty little twats stepped forward.

'Maybe you didn't hear me, I said, we, find you GUILTY'

He lunges for me, luckily my lightning-fast reflexes, and my nostrils sense he's coming at me so I effortlessly duck, I mean Jesus did none of these fuckers think to wash, oh that's good I should say that.

'Did none of you fuckers think to wash?'

That sounded better in my head somehow, I duck another punch from this pre-pubescent penis, one swift punch to the stomach and he goes down like a fifth of a ton of bricks, the guy's more wiry than the Joker before he gave up the crack.

'Hey Jean, I could really do with you waking up right now,' I yell frustratedly at her slumped body behind me as three more of these unwashed underdeveloped underlings come at me.

Ducking and diving has always come pretty easy to me: even before I got bitten by that spider I was a pro at Street Fighter 2 Turbo, but ever since then it's like I can sense danger coming towards me, it's like a sixth sense or something, and plus like *The Sixth Sense* I already know exactly what's going to happen – how did that film get past the spoiler-alert brigade? (I kick another of these little bitches in the head) I mean, I got my head torn off (not literally, although he could've done) by Boulderman when I mentioned about Eddard Stark being killed, and yet people yell *The Sixth Sense*'s twist from the rooftops as if it doesn't matter. Does that seem right to you?

I duck under the legs of one ass-faced assailant, throwing him casually into the two running at me. It's like these guys were trained in a church youth club; I'm not even sure you could call them villains, let alone supervillains. I wonder if I'll get extra points from Ms Apellio if I bring all 12 of these hoodlums to justice... I sweep the legs of another, not sure how I'd go about tying up 12 children and still seem like the good guy in this, huh, there's a warm tingling sensation in my back... is that? Oh. Yeah, that feels like a stun gun. I hit the floor pretty hard, urgh, and as my senses go numb I see this pizza-face kid standing over me, smiling.

'I'm going to tell your parents about this,' I slur before the world goes black.

CHAPTER THIRTEEN – (JUDGE, JURY, HOPEFULLY NO EXECUTIONER)

As I regain consciousness we're in some kind of medieval dungeon in chains. Jean is slumped next to me, still unconscious.

'Oh, way to bow down to gender stereotypes Jean, I could really do with you breaking with tradition, taking charge of the situation and using your powers to save me right now!' I bark at her in frustration.

'I'm afraid even if she were to wake, she'd be no use to you.' A deep and menacing voice comes from the shadows.

'Err... oh hello there, could you help me? I appear to have accidentally chained myself to the wall...' I try.

'Yes, Mr....' he glances down at something in his hand 'Arachno, is it?' As he steps out of the shadows I see this beast of a man, seven feet tall, built like a brick shit-house, dressed in sweeping red robes and wearing the most ridiculous wig I've ever seen, all curly and grey. Suddenly it clicks in my head.

'Oh, I get it... they were The Jury, so that makes you...'

'The Judge, yes, how very astute of you. My Jury have taken the liberty of providing you both with state of the art superpower dampening collars so there'll be no funny business, the only way to shut them down is of course this large button which I have hilariously installed on the other side of the room, exactly one metre further away from you than your chains will allow, because I am an evil genius. At 12 o'clock precisely the court will be brought to order and your trial for crimes against criminals will begin.'

As he walks out I slyly flick him the 'V's, it doesn't help the situation but it makes me feel a little better. Crimes against criminals? Is this guy for real? I give Jean a shake.

'Oi,' I whisper. 'Get up.' I shake her a bit harder, she slowly opens her eyes.

'Oh no,' she groans, 'we didn't have sex did we?'

'How very rude! I'll have you know both the girls that I've had sex with have remembered it happening!' ...That probably didn't make me sound as good as I was hoping.

'So what's going on?' she groggily asks.

'Well, it appears we've been captured by someone called The Judge, and at 12 o'clock we're going to have some kind of get together to decide whether we die or not, I'm paraphrasing him of course.'

'Oh no! Not The Judge, rumour has it that for every bad guy you've put in jail you get a lashing!' Jean says, suddenly panicked awake.

Hmm... technically I think I've put away, maybe seven bad guys? I'll probably be alright; but by the look on Jean's face she's been doing a thoroughly bloody good job, which won't work out well for her.

'We need to get out of here, like right now, if not sooner,' she blurts.

'Yeah, unfortunately, evil genius that The Judge is, he's put these superpower dampeners on us and put the button to switch them off a metre further away than these chains will let us get to, he's really thought of everything.'

Jean takes off her shoe and throws it at the button, our collars instantly falling off.

'Evil genius my ass.'

I pull off our chains using my suddenly returned super strength

'Right, let's get out of here,' Jean says looking at me. 'What's the plan?'

'Plan? Err... well how about you take us back in time?'

'To back when we were chained up? Or before to when we were captured? I have no idea how long we've been here but I'm guessing it's already been a few hours meaning that's a fucktard of an idea.'

'Once again, rude! Ok, well then looks like we fight our way out and escape injustice.'

'Okay, I really like your candour.' She would've loved my earlier candour, maybe I'll try and candour at someone on the way out.

As I head towards the door to start kicking some ass she apprehensively asks 'Two?'

'Technically two and a half... I wasn't a popular teenager. I don't want to talk about it. Let's kick some butt!'

CHAPTER FOURTEEN – (A FIGHT SCENE IN A BOOK)

'So there's 12 of them right?' Jean asks.

'Yeah, I think so; there might be a few alternates kicking about. Oh, and The Judge of course.'

Right, so just probably 15 to 20 guys, all between us and freedom, I really hope today's re-run of *Family Feud* is a shit one. Concentrate Arachno, this is no longer just about you: I need to make sure this girl is safe – that should be the only thing that matters.

'Let's do this,' I say as sturdily as I can. One last nod to each other and I kick open the door to the dungeon, knocking down the guard standing behind it. I think I should probably feel bad and then I remember these little fuckers tasered me in the back like a bunch of punks, I grab the little fucker and slam him against the wall. I wonder if I could get away with using the phrase 'hung jury'. It'd probably come out a bit too harsh. Two more minions come running round the corner, swiftly into my boot, and out of the corner of my eye I see Miss Strumper roundhousing a guy to the ground. That girl has serious moves; maybe she'll let me train with her some time.

'Four down,' I say. 'Looks like we're heading for a ...hung jury.' I see Jean's face wince – should've stuck with my first instinct really. I elbow another Juror in the face who tries to sneak up behind me, and fumble an apology to Jean as we head up the stairs. She waves me off dismissively.

As I reach the top of the stairs I see Jean panting heavily, standing over six Jurors, all beaten to a pulp.

'How did you...?'

'Time travel, baby. It's much easier to predict what someone's going to do when you've seen them do it twice already!' she smirks smugly.

Such a cheater, I really feel her power gives her an unfair advantage, then I remember I can climb up walls and let her off.

'So how often do you time travel without anyone noticing? Just out of interest? I mean surely it makes life seem a lot longer? Do you feel the time pull? Are you going to get older much sooner because you've technically been living a lot longer than the rest of us?'

'That's a lot of questions. Okay, so basically: time, it's sort of elastic, so when I time travel it's like an elastic band that stretches forward then pulls me back, so although I have experienced that time, because it hasn't happened, it doesn't count, so I don't get older because as the world resets itself it resets me as well, except I can remember what happened and use it to my advantage. And no, I haven't ever used it in a casino or used it to bring back someone from the dead.'

'How did you know I was going to ask....?'

'Is that a serious question? TIME TRAVELLER HERE! This is the fourth time we've had this conversation, but the first time your brain hasn't melted at the possibilities and hopefully we can continue now? Or do I have to reverse time again so you know to hold up your arm... now.'

I raise my arm as requested just as a Juror runs up and I absent mindedly clothesline him and he falls back down the stairs. I have to admit, it's a very useful power she's got there.

'But, how come sometimes we both travel and sometimes it's just you?' I ask trying not to sound like a complete idiot.

'You only come with me if I'm touching you, Arachno; keep up will you!' She snaps at me as though I'm a complete idiot.

A door opens in the next room, I grab Jean and climb up the wall and on to the ceiling above the door. The Judge enters the room with all the grace of a cement mixer. I mean, seriously, this guy makes the Rhino seem like a ballet dancer. Plus he's still wearing that wig. It makes me nostalgic for the good old days when supervillains were cool. Okay, maybe cool is the wrong word, but you could at least take them seriously.

'What in God's name is happening here? Pete!' He barks at one of the floored Jurors.

As this Pete starts to stir and mumble an apology he turns over to see me and Jean hanging above the Judge's head. He tries to stutter a dazed warning to his boss, but it's too late. I jump onto his head, obscuring his vision as Jean goes for his legs.

'Let's get rid of this ridiculous thing,' I say as I grab his wig and pull. It doesn't come off. What is this, glued to his head? I give it another tug, a bit of hair comes off in my hand and I hear The Judge yelp. It dawns on me: this isn't a wig.

'This isn't a wig? You purposely made your hair look like this? What is wrong with you?' I exclaim.

Just then Jean takes out his legs and we both go crashing to the ground, his fists flying ferociously as we tumble, cracking Jean right in the face and knocking her down. I use my spiderlike agility to jump to my feet, only to have The Judge's boot find my chest, hard, and send me flying across the room.

'Time for the bug to go splat,' The Judge spits, as he gets back to his feet and stomps over to me.

His shadow obscuring the light as he towers over me, he raises his fist for the final blow. Luckily, I manage to use my spiderlike cowardice to crawl under his legs and out of the way, just as his fist makes contact with the wall. He bellows in agony as brick meets bone. I grab Jean who is still lying on top of a few unconscious Jurors.

'Do me a favour, don't ever take me back to that moment, it was pretty terrifying' I whisper to her as I carry her towards the door, I throw it open but as we cross the threshold, standing in front of us in a 12-foot exoskeleton is The Dish, and he looks pissed.

'Steal my woman, will you? You Dish-honour me!' he yells, before maniacally laughing as he reveals his metal robot arms, one with a spinning plate, the other with a mace. Well now, this is just the worst timing. Not a bad quip to be fair to him, but really terrible timing.

CHAPTER FIFTEEN – (WHERE NO ONE GIVES ME A BREAK)

'Ah give me a break, Dish! We've got nothing in the books for today!' I yell, hoping he can hear me over all the wurrs and clunks his new suit is making. It looks pretty sweet to be fair to him: nice dark blue colour, what looks like rockets on the feet, although knowing The Dish, they probably don't work. They're probably just for show, and if he wasn't trying to kill me right now I'd probably ask whether they're even connected to the suit. I slowly back away still holding Jean, but unfortunately my escape route is blocked by a large man in a black dress, with a big clump of his ridiculous looking hair missing.

As The Dish raises his arm and fires a plate at me I duck and it smashes in to The Judge behind me, slightly winding him. I can see why The Dish would've gone for this, but it's not the most deadly of weapons.

'Who's this guy, The Arachno? Your new girlfriend? Nice wig, Grandad!' Dish yells at him.

'I wouldn't mock his hair if I were you,' I try to communicate, but it's too late: The Judge has seen red and charges towards The Dish in a berserker rage. I try to grab The Judge before he flattens Dish but he just drags me along behind him as he rugby tackles Dish to the ground. As I try to get my bearings back I see The Judge going for the finishing blow. I grab his fist and toss him off... I should probably rephrase that. I pull him off... that's not better. I throw him off Dish, but then as I turn towards The Judge I feel something incredibly solid hit the back of my head. It's The Dish's mace, and it properly knocks me for six. The world spins for a while and I decide it might be a good idea to fall down. Dish gets back up and goes straight after The Judge, but The Judge just grabs the robot arm with the mace attached to it and jerks it off. No comment.

'What the...' Dish stutters in surprise, staring down at his exposed arm in disbelief. 'How did he...' He looks round just in time to see a massive fist flying towards his face.

I've always had this dream where two girls are fighting over me, and in my dream that's always pretty nice. Two guys fighting over me, however, doesn't seem to hit the same level of joy for some reason. Probably due to the lack of bikinis and jelly. Actually I'm not sure that would improve this particular situation. I feel like I should be doing something right now but I just have this woozy feeling and quite blurred vision, and as I look up it seems something else has blocked out the sun. Whatever it is, it seems pretty angry at me... Oh I remember now: I was fighting those guys, yeah, that's probably one of them standing over me. I should probably do something. As my dazed hand tries to make a fist and half heartedly swing at the big blur above me, everything goes incredibly white, like the whole world has been covered in whipped cream. Then everything does dark.

CHAPTER SIXTEEN – (THE NEXT DAY)

As I open my eyes I don't recognise this place. It's all very clean, not like my apartment at all. There are some flowers and a balloon on the table next to me. As I look around it dawns on me: I'm in a hospital room, urgh how cliché. I turn over and see Ms Strumper sitting reading a magazine.

'Urflurghushluf,' I say, not entirely sure what it was I was going for.

'Ah! You're awake! Man I wish I could time travel into the future, turns out sitting by someone's bedside is really, really boring! Your friend Steve has been here literally the whole time. He's just gone to get a drink. He's lovely... a bit annoying, but lovely.

'What... what happened?' I try to ask as comprehensively as possible.

'Well while you were having fun getting slapped around, I followed procedure and called in the SIA for backup. They showed up just in time to stop The Judge from smashing your face into the floor. He's been taken into custody along with The Dish. They shouldn't be a problem until they escape from prison, but that normally takes at least a few weeks, so it'll give you some time to recover.'

Just then the door bursts open and in walks Kristine Appellio 'Well! Here's something I thought I'd never see. Mr Arachno, going after two supervillians at the same time? I mean I thought you had no balls, like none at all, but it turns out they're massive. When push comes to shove, you have gigantic balls, and I respect a man with huge balls.'

'Thank you?' I ask.

'You're welcome. This is some great work, and following protocol to the letter, calling for back up but trying to hold them off to reduce civilian casualties, and at the same time protecting a fellow superhero? This will be front page news tomorrow. You've really put the agency in a good light; I'm very proud. Although if you had've attended a few more classes you might not have gotten beaten so bad, but all the same well done for your first high profile fight. This was a win in the eyes of the agency.' And with that she was gone.

'I think that's the first time I've ever seen that frigid woman smile.' I say in disbelief. 'Hey, why didn't you take credit for calling back up?'

'Well, you just seemed so helpless I figured you needed a win. And to show you why we do things by the book,' she smiles condescendingly but sweetly.

Things by the book eh? Yeah, maybe there is something in it, I mean yeah, I got my arse handed to me, but at least I put my arse out there, y'know? Maybe I should be trying a bit harder. It feels pretty good to know someone is proud of me, plus it'd probably do wonders for my profile, maybe even get a sponsor, then I could actually afford to buy some stuff, like nice food, maybe a spare costume. This one is pretty fucked now.

'Hey,' I say, 'do you fancy teaching me a few of your moves?'

'Yeah, sure, once you get better, plus you should really start going to the seminars at the agency: they're pretty useful.'

'Maybe I will, maybe I will...'

So maybe I'm not the greatest superhero, certainly not the most well known, or the most competent, but with a little bit of training, motivation and help from friends I guess that you could say, justice, the word alone, is, ah no wait, the expression alone? Ah fuck it.

Printed in Great Britain
by Amazon